The Listening Silence

PHYLLIS ROOT
The Listening Silence

paintings by
DENNIS McDERMOTT

HarperCollins*Publishers*

Library of Congress Cataloging-in-Publication Data

Root, Phyllis.

The listening silence / by Phyllis Root ; paintings by Dennis
McDermott.

p.   cm.

Summary: A young Indian girl triumphs over her fears and proves
herself worthy to be the mystical healer of her village.

ISBN 0-06-025092-5. — ISBN 0-06-025093-3 (lib. bdg.)

[1. Healers—Fiction.   2. Indians of North America—Fiction.]
I. McDermott, Dennis, ill.   II. Title.

PZ7.R6784Li   1992   90-37425

[Fic]—dc20   CIP

                                                                  AC

For Sandra, who listens,
and Marion, who believed
in Kiri and me.
—P.R.

In the silence I wait,
In the silence I listen.

PROLOGUE

▶▶◆◀◀

Kiri waited alone in the silence of the winter tent. Somewhere outside the tent a korlu called. Kiri let a part of her mind drift free, beyond the skins and furs stretched tightly over tent poles, until she was *within* the bird.

Her throat tightened as she called, *Korlu, korlu.* Her wings stretched as she took flight above the deep, drifted snow. Beating against the cold, still air, she circled up over the trees and out toward the frozen lake. Nothing moved in the whiteness below.

As easily as she had slipped *within*, Kiri left the bird and was back in the tent, alone and waiting.

"Stay inside until I return," her mother had told her when she left. "Your father has been gone two days now, and may be hurt. When I have found him, I will come back to you. You will be safe here,

1

my little hunter." She had hugged Kiri fiercely and kissed the top of her head. Lacing the tent flap shut behind her, Kiri's mother had gone.

Bundled in her furs, Kiri had waited, chewing the dried-meat strips her mother had left and playing with the story beads her father had carved in the long winter nights. A storm shook the skins of the tent, but Kiri waited, safe and warm. When she heard the small sounds of some animal outside, she would go *within*, hoping to see through the animal's eyes what had become of her parents. Always she saw only frozen drifts and the snow-covered branches of trees.

When the voice came, it woke her from sleep.

Kiri, Kiri, the voice called, and she fumbled with the door flap of the tent before realizing that the voice was inside her.

Kiri, the voice called again.

"Mother!" Kiri cried. "Father, where are you?"

For an instant she was *within* her mother. Then a searing pain ran down Kiri's side and swept her away. Once more a voice cried in her mind, *Kiri, Kiri.* She struggled against the current of pain, back toward her mother's voice.

Silence.

A great, blinding whiteness filled Kiri's mind. The whiteness swallowed her up like the snow that sometimes filled the air, hiding light and shadow.

When the tent took shape around her again, Kiri did not know how much time had passed. She was cold and stiff, huddled on the tent floor. In her mind was a new silence. It filled the place where her mother's voice had spoken.

"Mother," she whispered. The word sank into silence like a warm stone dropped into snow. A coldness spread from Kiri's stomach out to her fingertips.

"They will come back for me," she said aloud. "I know they will."

Alone in the silence, Kiri waited. Another storm shook the tent. Night darkened around her, and daylight came again. When the sound of voices came muffled through the tent flap, Kiri called out eagerly, "I am here, Mother."

The door flap fell open, and bright sunlight splashed into the tent.

"May we enter?" asked a voice that Kiri did not know. Two people crawled inside. Their faces were the faces of strangers. Kiri crouched back against the tent skins.

"It's a child," one of the strangers, a woman, said. "Five winters old, perhaps." She held out her hand to Kiri. "Where are your parents?"

Kiri recognized the words that the woman spoke.

3

But she clutched her story beads and stared silently.

"Perhaps they are hunting," the second stranger, a man, said.

"We saw no tracks nearby," the woman answered, "and we are far from any village." She turned back to Kiri. "We will wait with you for your people to return, if we may."

The man frowned. "The village needs meat," he argued, "and we are hunters, not watchers of children. This child is not even one of our people."

"All people were once one people, and still are," the woman replied, "even though we are scattered over the bones of the earth. So the song says." Her voice was soft like Kiri's mother's, although her face was veined with wrinkles. "Do you know this song?" she asked Kiri.

Kiri nodded. In her mind she could hear her father's voice singing as his fingers traced the story beads. Somewhere at the edges of her memory she recalled other faces, other people besides her parents. But they were shadows in the firelight, like the people in the stories her father sang about. For many moons the only people Kiri had known had been her mother and father, hunting together and gathering the grain that ripened on swaying stalks around the marshy edges of the lakes.

"We will wait with you," the woman said again. "I am Ana, and my companion is Yaro."

The man did not argue. Kiri was silent, too. She could not make the strangers leave. But she would not give them her name.

For three days Ana and Yaro waited with Kiri, and still her parents did not return. Yaro was often gone hunting. But Ana stayed with Kiri, and because the woman spoke gently, Kiri came to her at last and whispered how her father had gone out to hunt and had not come back. How her mother had left to search for him, telling Kiri to wait.

"You cannot wait forever," Ana said, "and our village is hungry for the meat we bring." She smoothed a strand of hair off Kiri's forehead and said, "We will take you with us."

"I have to stay!" Kiri cried, wrenching herself away from Ana. "They are coming back for me."

"I know, little one, they will come back," Ana soothed her. "We will leave a message for them. Then they will come to our village and find you, and you will be with them again."

From the fire-circle Ana took a charred stick and drew a line of pictures on the wall of the tent, showing how she and Yaro had found the tent, and Kiri, and how they were taking her to their village. Kiri stared at the pictures Ana drew, tracing them with her finger not quite touching. There was a pattern to them that she had seen before.

"That is the way to our village," Ana told her. "Those are the lakes, and the trails between them."

"I know," Kiri answered. "I see them sometimes when I am a bird."

Ana looked at her curiously. "And are you other things besides a bird?" she asked.

Kiri nodded.

"In our village," Ana said, "only Mali can see through the eyes of another. He would be glad of your coming. You are welcome to stay with us until your parents return."

So Kiri rolled up her bedskin, took her story beads, and followed Ana and Yaro through the snow. She turned back often to see if her parents were coming behind. Only the wind followed, blowing snow across her tracks.

For five days they traveled slowly, sleeping in their bedskins at night, turning from the trail to follow the tracks of animals. When Ana killed a derek, the song she and Yaro sang as they skinned it was the same one Kiri's parents had often sung.

At the end of the fifth day they came to the village across a frozen lake. Darkness was closing over the sky. Kiri's feet were numb, and the wind spit ice in her face. When Ana stopped suddenly, Kiri stumbled into her.

Cupping her hands around her mouth, Ana shouted, and Yaro took up the call. Kiri peered

around Ana, but all she saw were trees crowding the shores of the lake.

Then a light flickered among the trees, and another. People came out onto the ice carrying torches, more people than Kiri had ever seen in her life. She clung to Ana's legs, but Ana was laughing and waving to the strangers.

"Three derek!" Yaro called.

"Three derek and a child!" Ana said as she lifted Kiri up in her arms. Strange faces crowded in around Kiri. She buried her face in Ana's furs.

But she could not shut out the noise. People gathered in a strange round tent where babies cried, children shouted, and men and women scolded and laughed. The only familiar thing was the smell of derek stew simmering over the fire. Kiri tried to eat, but her stomach had tightened into a knot. She curled up against Ana and closed her eyes. The voices surrounded her. She heard Ana telling how she and Yaro had found the tent in the forest, and Kiri in it.

"Mali," Ana said, "you will want to talk with this one. She sees with the eyes of a bird."

"I think she is a bird tonight," a soft voice answered. "A frightened little bird that has fallen from its nest." A hand rested on Kiri's head, and a warmth washed through her.

Mother, she thought sleepily, Father. Tomorrow they will come for me.

But the morning was filled with more strangers. In the daylight Kiri could see all the small, round dwellings tucked among the trees. She had slept the night with Ana in one of them.

Ana led her along a path to the place where they had eaten the night before. "The common wellan," she told Kiri. In the daylight Kiri could see how it was made of bent saplings woven with reeds.

She followed Ana inside. People crowded together in the wellan, scooping food out of bowls. Kiri's skin tightened. The air was full of people, too full. She tugged on Ana's hand, but Ana had turned to speak to someone. A boy grabbed Kiri's arm.

Kiri tried to pull away. There was a darkness about the boy, cold and hard as stone.

"What are you called?" the boy asked. "Where are your people? Why are you here?"

"Leave her be, Garen." A hand reached out and seized the boy, fingers digging into his shoulder. Kiri saw Yaro's face behind Garen as Garen flushed.

Her own shoulder ached suddenly. Kiri yanked her arm free and ran outside. Ana's voice called after her, but Kiri kept running. The forest would hide her. She would not go back to the village full of noise and strangers. She would find her way back to the tent where her parents had left her. She would wait there until they came for her.

It was quiet among the trees. Kiri let the silence fill her up. Her feet made a path in the snow. Which way was her parents' tent?

"They will find me," she said out loud. "I will wait here for them." Crouching down by a rock, she felt in the pouch tied to her belt for her story beads. Her fingers moved along the beads until she found the one carved like a werrel. If she closed her eyes, she could see her father's hands carefully shaping the werrel's round body and long ears.

He had carved the bead after killing a werrel. From its skin her mother had made warm mittens for Kiri. Kiri remembered the soft whisper of fur against her skin when she held them to her face. As her father carved, he had sung of the werrel's death and the new mittens.

Holding the bead, Kiri sang his words softly, "Black eye in white snow, come, come to me. Warm my little one. . . ."

A hand touched her shoulder. Kiri opened her eyes to see a man kneeling beside her. A woven red band held his long gray hair back from his forehead. His voice when he spoke was the same voice she had heard the night before.

"I am Mali," he said. "And you are the little lost bird."

"I'm not a bird," Kiri told him.

"But sometimes you are a bird, aren't you?" he asked gently.

Kiri's fingers tightened on the story beads. She nodded.

"It is not an easy gift, to see with another's eyes," Mali told her. "I know. It is my gift, too. Come stay with me and I will teach you the uses of your gift."

Kiri shook her head. "My parents are coming for me."

"Stay with me until they come," Mali said.

He was beside her, a stranger; yet he did not trouble the stillness of the trees. She would be safe with him until her parents came. Kiri put her fingers into his outstretched hand and followed him back through the forest to the village.

"What are you called?" he asked as they walked.

"I am Kiri," she answered.

*I sing, and the sun hears
my song and answers.*

1

"Center of light, circle of the day, arise."

The power of the sun-rejoicing sang in Kiri. She lowered her arms as the last words echoed across the lake and the sun broke free of the trees.

"It was well sung," Mali told her, and Kiri gathered up his words like bright pebbles to keep. Moon after moon, for eight long circles of the sun, she had followed Mali down to the singing rock to help him call the sun into the sky. For many days now, since the beginning of the moon of squash ripening, he had let her sing alone.

A pair of tenabi skimmed low over the lake, wings spread, long necks outstretched, blue-green feathers gleaming. Kiri's heart lifted. It was a day to take wing and fly. She entered *within* one of the tenabi.

Water rushed around her in little waves as she

landed on the lake. Her mate cried out to her as he circled nearby. Beneath the water's surface she could see silver fish darting away.

"Kiri." Mali's voice pulled her back from the bird. "It is not a morning to spend your power on tenabi. Nikil is in need of healing. We must go to her after first meal."

A cloud shadowed the bright morning, and Kiri shivered.

"Must I come, too?" she asked Mali.

"You must," he told her. "You are thirteen winters old. That is old enough to begin to be singer for our people. *Within* a tenabe, *within* a person—it is not so different."

It is different, Kiri thought.

But she did not say the words out loud. Mali knew the terror that shook her whenever she was *within* a person. She could not hide it from him. He would not ask for her help in healing unless the need was great.

"I will try," she told him.

"Good." Mali smiled. "Come now, I smell corn soup and bread for first meal. After, we will go to Nikil."

Kiri held out her arm, and Mali took it, leaning against her as they started up the path to the village. Kiri's own legs ached with Mali's pain as they walked. Yet even in his pain he would go to Nikil to heal her. Kiri felt her face flood hot with

shame at her own fear. But the fear did not go away.

Inside the common wellan villagers sat on mats on the ground, eating. Most of the children old enough to walk crowded at one end of the circle, giggling and poking one another as they ate. One of them, Ebba, waved wildly at Kiri. The bowl balanced in Ebba's lap tilted and threatened to spill. Kiri smiled back, and Ebba grinned shyly and ducked her head, her dark hair standing out around her face like a cloud. Only four winters old, Ebba already knew most of the learning songs and many of the remembering songs.

Kiri helped Mali to sit down, then found a place for herself. Someone passed her a bowl of steaming soup and a flat circle of bread. Kiri took them, feeling the air close in around her. In all the years she had lived with the villagers, she had never grown used to so many people. All their fears, sorrows, aches pressed against her. Only alone in the forest could she find silence. Alone, or with Mali.

"It is part of your gift, part of what helps us to heal," Mali had told her once. He had taught her how to sort out the unspoken voices of the people around her. It helped, a little, to learn to listen to each separate voice.

Beside her she could feel her friend Tomar like a bowl of water, still and clear.

Mali's pain as he ate slowly, his fingers wrapped

16

around his bowl, was like a cramping in Kiri's own hands.

Ebba's happiness came in ripples.

Darkness brushed against Kiri. Garen, she thought.

She turned to see him bending over his bowl, his hair falling forward unbound. When he looked up and saw her watching him, he scowled and turned away. One hand reached out to touch the spear that he carried with him everywhere he went.

When she had first come to the village, Kiri had gone often into the forest, seeking silence *within* a werrel or a rock or a tree. Many times she had come back to herself to find Garen watching her. Always he would frown and slip away.

One day he had stayed, shifting from foot to foot.

"How do you do it?" he had blurted out at last, his fingers clenched. "How do you know where the animals are? How do you find them? If I could do that, I would be the best hunter in the village."

Kiri shrugged. "I feel it," she said, "like knowing a lake is close by, or rain is coming."

"Teach me," Garen said.

Kiri had shaken her head. "I can't. Mali says it is a gift."

Garen had stalked away.

Tomar nudged Kiri, brushing the memory aside. "Are you finished?" she asked.

Kiri nodded and wiped a last bite of bread around the smooth clay of her bowl. As they left the wellan, Kiri's shoulders began to unknot.

The open space around the common wellan was filled with small, tidy plots where the villagers grew beans, grain, and the round golden fruits called "full moon." Beans hung on the vines in long purple pods.

"Are you helping in the fields today?" Tomar asked.

"I cannot," Kiri answered. "Are you?"

Tomar grinned and shook her head, her long brown braid bouncing. Her delight blew through Kiri like a warm wind.

"This morning I must fire my pots," Tomar said. "The first time since my vision path." She reached up to touch the woven blue band around her forehead that marked her as a potter.

"Has Mali said when he will send you on your vision path?" Tomar asked.

Kiri shook her head. If her vision spoke and called her singer, the villagers would look to her to heal them. And she could not. But she could not tell even Tomar about the terror that shook her when she thought of healing. Only Mali knew what it was like to feel another's pain. And Mali, at least, could heal that pain. He was not swept away by it

18

into a great, white emptiness that swallowed people up forever. Her mother had gone into that emptiness, and Kiri had not been able to stop her. She shivered.

"I am not ready for my vision yet," she said. "There is still much I must learn."

They stopped in front of the small round wellan that Kiri and Mali shared.

"If I spent all my time learning," Tomar said, "we would not have any dishes to eat out of or bowls to carry water in." She laughed. "And if my firing fails, we will still have no dishes or bowls. I must hurry. Saba will be waiting. Go well, Kiri."

"Go well," Kiri told her. As Tomar walked on, Kiri felt her friend's gladness leaving with her. Soon Mali would come, and they would go to Nikil.

The wind in the forest called to Kiri. It would be green and quiet among the trees.

But Mali had asked for her help in healing Nikil. Mali, who had held Kiri and sung to her when she cried for the parents who did not come. Mali, who had taught her the names of trees and plants and rocks. Mali, whom she loved.

Kiri sat down before the wellan to wait for him. A weight settled in her chest, cold and heavy as a stone.

Only darkness, only silence.
Somewhere the wind is speaking.

2

When Kiri saw Mali coming slowly along the path, she ran to help him. Inside the wellan he opened several of the small bags hanging from the poles that held up the wellan's covering of skins. As he took out each dried leaf or root, he held it up for Kiri to name: feverleaf, ennis, bloodberry. She knew where each grew in the forest, and what time of year to gather it. Mali had taught her well, and she loved this kind of learning. He nodded at her answers and tucked the plants carefully into a pouch.

The weight of stone in Kiri's chest grew heavier as they made their way to Nikil's wellan. She wanted to take Mali's hand, a child of five winters again instead of thirteen. But he was leaning heavily against her. At Nikil's wellan he lifted the door flap. Kiri drew a shaky breath and followed him inside.

She could hear Nikil's breathing, thin and raspy.

Even though the day was growing warm, the hides that covered the wellan were rolled down to the ground. In the dim light Kiri could see deep lines in Nikil's face. The woman's hands lay limp against her blanket. Many days Kiri had sat beside Nikil in the sun, watching those hands weave patterns into belts and blankets and bands. Kiri wanted to touch Nikil's hands, comfort her, heal her. But already the air was pressing in on Kiri. She did not dare come any closer to Nikil and her pain.

Nikil tossed restlessly. Mali knelt and took her fingers in his own.

"Light a fire," he told Kiri, "and get out the fever-leaf, but do not put it on the flame until I tell you."

Kiri built a little pile of twigs, glad for something to do. With the firestone she carried in her belt pouch, she soon had a fire burning. Nikil's face looked pale in its flickering light. Mali was silent, his eyes closed, his breathing deep and even.

"Wind, hear my song," he began.

Kiri closed her eyes. She would try to follow Mali *within*.

"Wind, hear my name," she sang with him.

Nikil's pain burned through her like a strong, hot wind. Kiri clenched her fists. Around her an emptiness was opening, drawing her down into its still, white heart, down to where she must not go. Something waited for her in that white stillness.

From out of the silence a voice called, *Kiri, Kiri.*

22

Terror shook her.

"Mali!" she screamed.

She could feel him beside her, helping her. The wind died, the voice faded, the pain burned away.

Kiri's heart thudded as she opened her eyes. Mali still sat beside Nikil, his voice rising in song. His hands moved along Nikil's side.

Suddenly he threw back his head, his face tight. Nikil moaned softly. Pain sliced through Kiri's side and was gone.

"Now!" Mali's voice was sharp. Kiri's hands shook as she crumpled up the pointed leaves of the fever-leaf and sprinkled them over the flames. A thin, bitter smell filled the wellan. Nikil opened her eyes.

"The pain is gone," she whispered.

"You must rest now," Mali told her, laying his hand on her forehead. Nikil's eyes closed.

Mali sagged against Kiri as she helped him outside. He did not speak as they walked slowly back to their wellan. Kiri helped him to lie down, tucking a blanket close around him. It was a blanket Nikil had woven, dark with a pale stripe. It felt thick and warm under Kiri's fingers. Nikil would weave again because of Mali. But Kiri had failed Mali, and Nikil, too. She blinked away tears and rose to leave. She would let Mali sleep. But he reached out a hand. Kiri took his fingers in her own. His skin looked gray against her own brown palm.

"Mali, I'm sorry," she told him. "I tried to help. But there was too much pain."

His voice was faint, and she bowed her head to hear him. "You must find your own way through the pain," he told her. "At the center of the pain is the place where you will be able to heal." His fingers tightened on hers. "You must find that place, Kiri. The village will need you soon."

Kiri's chest closed like a fist.

"Mali," she whispered, "have you seen your death?"

He did not answer. His eyes closed, and his breathing grew deeper and slower. Kiri waited until his fingers relaxed in hers. Then she laid his hand down gently, pushed the door flap aside, and stepped outside.

A thin trail of smoke rose from the trees. Tomar's firing. In the clearing workers bent over the rows of plants, gathering the long purple bean pods to dry for winter food. Kiri knew she should go help with the harvest.

But Mali's words echoed in her mind. He was her rock, the center of her world. He would not die and leave her as her parents had left her.

She would not think about Mali dying. Alone among the trees, she could lose herself in a bird or rock or fish. *Within*, she would be safe from questions, from fears.

Kiri's feet moved toward the forest.

25

Even the stones are silent.
The rocks refuse to speak.

3

The wind in the branches soothed Kiri as she walked. She followed a path between trees and rocks where moss grew in patches of gray and green. Sunlight fell through the leaves.

Coming around a turn of the path, Kiri stopped suddenly. Garen was sitting beside the trail, half hidden by the trunk of a tree. He had not heard her. There was a stillness about him, as easy as the wind in the trees. In his hands he held a piece of wood. The head of a tenabe with its long bill and round eyes stared out of the wood at Kiri. Wings spread back from its shoulders feather by feather. With his long hunter's knife Garen carefully shaved away a sliver of wood from the beak.

Kiri stepped back. She did not want to see Garen now. She would go another way.

But a leaf crackled under her foot. Garen looked up.

A flush climbed his face when he saw her. He scowled down at the piece of wood in his hand, then threw it into the tall grass along the edge of the trail.

"It's beautiful," Kiri protested.

"It's only a scrap of wood," Garen muttered. He reached for the spear lying beside him and stood up. He was taller than Kiri, a winter older. When Garen had followed his vision path three months ago, no vision had spoken to him.

Brushing past Kiri, he disappeared in the forest. The air lightened after he left.

Kiri went a different way, following the sound of water to where a tiny stream splashed over rocks. It was cool and peaceful by the stream. Silence surrounded her. She settled herself on the ground, leaning against the solid comfort of a tree.

A sudden movement across the stream broke the stillness. A brown flick of ear, a quick hop, and a werrel was below her, drinking from the stream. Kiri smiled and went *within*.

Cool water slipped down her throat. Her ears caught the sound of grass bending in the wind. She smelled wet earth, and green leaves, and something else, somewhere, a menace. . . .

Pain tore through her.

Kiri leaped to her feet and whirled around as the

werrel disappeared in a tangle of leaves. A spear quivered in the earth where the werrel had been.

Garen stood on a rock behind Kiri.

He must have followed her. Kiri's voice shook as she said, "You had no right."

"The right of a hunter to find food for the village," Garen returned.

"The village has no need of meat, and you are no hunter," Kiri retorted. "No vision spoke to you."

Garen scowled. "Yaro will send me again soon to seek my vision path," he told her. "Then you will see."

His anger washed over Kiri as he pushed past her to pull his spear from the ground. Under the anger Kiri could feel the werrel's pain. She shuddered. Somewhere in the bushes the werrel lay bleeding. She stood, waiting. She would not lead Garen to the werrel.

But he did not even search for it.

"You'll see," he told Kiri again as he stalked off into the trees.

Kiri waited until Garen had gone, then waded across the stream. She found the werrel lying on its side in a clump of bushes. Kiri knelt down, but before she could touch the werrel, the pupils of its eyes went round and clear like wide, black pools.

It was not a good death. There had been no talk between hunter and hunted—no life asked for, no life given. The werrel had not been ready to die.

There would be no strength for anyone in its meat, nor warmth in its fur. Garen had not even sung the death song for it.

Kiri laid one hand on the werrel's soft fur and sang,

> "The strength of your life you have given.
> The courage of your death you have given.
> With thanks I receive them,
> With thanks I accept them.
> We are one, you and I,
> We are one."

She waited until a small wind blew through the trees and was still. The day was full of death— Mali's talk of dying, the werrel's death. What if Mali were dying now? Suddenly she wanted only to be back with him, watching his chest rise and fall with each breath, waiting for him to awaken. Garen had taken away any peace she might find in the forest. Kiri turned toward the village.

As she passed the spot where she had seen Garen, she looked in the grass for his carving, but she could not find it.

For three days Mali lay in the wellan, resting. Always he was tired after a healing, but Kiri had never seen him so weak. She brought him his food and sat beside him while he slept. On the third morning he was well enough to send her to gather pela berries for the winter. Bitter to eat, the berries were useful for curing stomachaches. Kiri took a basket and set off into the forest.

She found a patch of pela bushes, the branches bending with small red berries, and filled her basket. Mali would be pleased. Unless the whole village came down with aching stomachs, the berries would last until spring.

As she opened the door flap of the wellan, Kiri heard voices. Harga, chief elder of the village, was talking with Mali. They fell silent as Kiri came into the wellan. She reached for the drying baskets to spread the berries in the sun, but Mali held up his hand.

"Go find other elders first," he told her. "Tell them they must meet here tonight."

"What is it?" she asked.

He shook his head. "I will talk with you after they meet," he told her.

Kiri's hand shook a little as she set the berry basket down. What was so serious that the elders must meet? Was Mali worse?

She found Ana first, working with the harvesters.

"What is wrong, Kiri?" Ana asked. "You look troubled."

"Mali says the elders must meet at our wellan tonight," Kiri told her. "But he doesn't say why."

Ana set down her basket and stood up.

32

"I will tell the others for you," she said. Her hand rested briefly on Kiri's shoulder. "Try not to worry," Ana said, and set off to find the other elders.

Maybe work would take her mind off of worrying. Kiri picked up the basket Ana had left and began to fill it. It calmed her to feel the long, smooth pods, knotty with the seeds hidden inside.

"Kiri," a young man named Yolan called to her. "Give us a song to help with the harvest." The baby bound to Yolan's back with a wide strip of cloth stirred and opened its eyes, then nestled down to sleep again.

Kiri raised her voice in a harvest song, and up and down the rows other voices took up the words. Ebba set down the small basket she was working to fill and came to crouch beside Kiri, watching her face while she sang. Kiri smiled back at her.

Mali was only tired from healing Nikil, she told herself. Soon he would be well again.

Kiri did not return to the wellan after last meal. The singing rock still held a little of the day's warmth, and she waited there, shivering when the breeze blew off the water. One by one stars crept into the sky.

"Kiri!" Harga's voice called to her. "Mali will speak with you now."

Kiri rubbed her palms up and down her legs to

33

warm them as she walked back to the wellan. A small fire flickered inside. Mali was waiting for her alone.

"The elders have heard me," he told her. "They have spoken. You must leave to follow your vision path as soon as you can be ready."

A shaking started deep inside of Kiri. She wrapped her arms tightly around her middle to keep the shaking still.

"Now?" she protested. "It's almost winter." Spring was the time for vision paths, or summer.

"The village may have need of you soon," he told her. "I may not see the spring."

"Let me stay," she pleaded. "Who will take care of you?"

"Tomar will come," he said. "You must find your vision and learn your name. A singer is the voice of the village, to call the rains to our fields, the fish to our nets, the winds to our healings. You know this. If the voice of the people is silent, the crops will be poor and the people will sicken."

Kiri bowed her head, but the shaking inside her did not stop. How could she leave Mali?

Mali reached out and took her hands. His fingers felt cold against her own.

"Little one," he said gently, "I would wait to send you if I could, but the need of the people is great."

"What will my vision say?" she whispered.

34

"I cannot tell you," Mali answered. "You must go, and listen, and come back to tell me."

Mali's fingers loosened their hold, and he lay back against the bedskins. "Harga will help you prepare for the journey," he told her. "You go alone, but not alone."

"What do you mean?" Kiri asked.

Mali's eyes closed. The firelight threw shadows on his face. Kiri saw that he was sleeping. She tucked the bedskins closer around him.

But she could not sleep. Fear crowded up in her throat. She slipped outside. The winter constellations were beginning to rise. The hunter, the werrel, the abar crept low against the horizon.

Mali won't die, she thought fiercely. I won't let him.

If she must follow her vision path, she would go quickly and return soon. She would care for Mali when winter came. When the sun warmed the earth again in spring, he would not speak of dying.

Kiri fumbled for her story beads. One was carved like the faces of the moon, and Kiri held it in her fingers. For an instant the walls of the winter tent rose up around her, and she heard again her father's voice.

"Frost moon, hungry moon, story moon, comes the cold, comes the time of sleeping. . . ."

Kiri sang the words to herself, but they did not

comfort her. In the moon of cold her parents had left her, and she had not been able to help them. Now Mali talked of dying. She could not bear to lose him, too, to be alone again.

She held the bead, telling herself the story. When the wanderer's star climbed above the dark edge of trees, Kiri went back into the wellan, the taste of salt in her mouth.

Somewhere the korlu calls.

Is it my name I hear?

4

All day while she gathered supplies, Kiri argued with Harga. When Harga packed food enough for two moons, Kiri unpacked it.

"Take it, Kiri," Harga urged. "Winter is a hungry time. You may be gone longer than you think."

"Others travel lightly on their vision paths," Kiri insisted. "So will I."

Many of the paths between lakes and rivers were rocky and steep. She would have to carry the abar and all her supplies along them. Too much weight would only slow her down.

While Harga was busy with other tasks, Kiri unpacked the food, keeping only a small supply of meal cakes and dried meat. Besides the food and her bedskins, she took only the story beads her father had carved.

A footstep behind her made her turn. Garen was

coming across the narrow beach, his arms loaded with a bedskin and two hunting spears. Mali had told her this morning that the elders were sending Garen, too.

"He wants to go with the hunters this winter, and he cannot until he finds his path," Mali had said.

"Will he find it this time?" Kiri had asked.

"To find his vision, he must heal himself," Mali had answered. "If he cannot listen to the voice of his vision this time, he will have need of me—or of you. You know the story of Olin."

Kiri nodded. Olin had followed his vision path but would not listen for his vision. When he returned to the village, whatever he turned his hands to came to nothing. The abars he built cracked and leaked; the crops he tended withered. Before the moon of deep snows, Olin himself had sickened beyond healing.

Garen dumped his load into one of the abars pulled up on the sand and turned to Kiri. "I will come back soon, a hunter," he said proudly.

"Are you so sure your vision will tell you what you want to hear?" Kiri asked.

Garen's eyes darkened. "I will be the best hunter in the village," he told her. "Yaro has said so." He turned away.

Kiri could feel the little flicker of fear inside of Garen as he walked away. Fear of what? That his vision might not speak to him? Or that it might not name him hunter?

What would her own vision say? Would it name her singer and send her back to the villagers to take on their pains and sicknesses? Would it give her the courage to heal? Or would it name her with another name?

Kiri's fingers tightened into fists. Maybe her vision would name her a maker of abars or pots, or a grower of food. She would be safe, then, safe from the empty stillness that called her name.

Someone tugged at her hand. Kiri uncurled her fingers, and a small hand slid into hers. Ebba stood beside her. Kiri shoved away her thoughts of visions and knelt beside Ebba.

"What treasure did you find this time?" Kiri asked her.

Ebba held out her hand. In her small brown palm lay a piece of rock that caught the sunlight and broke it into slivers.

"It is a finger bone of the earth," Kiri said. "You are very lucky to find it."

"The tenabe showed me where to look," Ebba said proudly.

"You did well to listen," Kiri told her.

Ebba grinned happily and carefully closed her fingers around her stone. She skipped over to the abar and touched the bedskin rolled up in the bottom. "Will you be gone long?" she asked.

Kiri shook her head. "I will come back soon and teach you new songs."

"I will watch for you," Ebba said. She threw her arms around Kiri in a tight hug. Kiri hugged her back. Ebba, Mali, Tomar—she would leave them all behind while she followed her vision path. When she came back to the village, who would she be?

A sudden thought made her catch her breath.

If she came back a healer, could she heal Mali?

That night Kiri dreamed of a wide lake ruffled by wind. It was a lake so wide that the far shore was only a dark line between water and sky. The edges of the waves foamed and frayed and broke white on the water.

Kiri, the voices called across the dream water. *Kiri.*

"Where are you?" she cried, stretching out her hands. But the wind caught her words and flung them away, caught up the sand and whirled it into her eyes so that tears ran down her cheeks.

Still the voices called, *Kiri, Kiri.*

Kiri awoke, the dream vivid in her mind. She could not remember who had called her name or why. Then the walls of the wellan took shape in the pale darkness before dawn. She could see Mali sleeping, his breath rising in little white puffs.

Kiri pulled her blanket closer against the dream voices and the chilly air. Already the moon of water freezing was beginning to grow in the sky. Yesterday when she had gone to sing the sun-rejoicing, Kiri had found brittle pockets of ice in little hollows of the rock.

Mali, what will you do when the snows come? she thought.

Slipping out from under her blanket, she tucked it gently around Mali, then quickly pulled on her tunic and leggings and thick hide boots. She would leave as soon as she sang the sun into the sky. To say good-bye to Mali was more than she could bear.

Tomar stood waiting for her at the edge of the lake, a smooth black bowl in her hands.

"Here." She held it out. "From my first firing. Take it with you to remember that I am watching over Mali until you come back."

Words caught in Kiri's throat, and she hugged her friend.

"Go well, Kiri," Tomar said. Then she turned and walked away toward the village.

Kiri tucked the bowl inside the bedskins in her abar. As she stepped out onto the singing rock, a chill wind blew across her face so that she stumbled over the first words of the song. As the sun leaped free of the trees and the echo of her own voice died away, Kiri could hear the villagers gathering for first meal.

Even the wellan crowded with people felt more welcome than the vision path stretching before her. But the vision path waited. It was time to be gone.

With a single motion Kiri pushed her abar out into the lake and jumped in. As she reached for her paddle, something sparkled in the bottom of the abar. Ebba's stone. Kiri picked it up, feeling the smooth surface and the rough, sand-coated ends. Had Ebba forgotten it here? Or was it, like Tomar's bowl, a gift?

Kiri tucked the stone into her belt pouch. She could give it back to Ebba in a few days when she returned.

By the time Kiri paddled to the end of the lake, the sun had risen high. A gap in the trees showed the path to the next lake. This land was familiar to her. She had come here often with Mali to learn the places where tenabi nested in summer and derek fed in winter. As she shouldered her abar, she thought of Mali's last words to her the night before.

"I think you must go far," he had told her. "Here, where you know the land, you will also hear the voices that you know. It may be harder for you to listen for the voice of your vision."

She did not stop for midmeal but paddled all day. The sun was almost touching the tops of the trees when she pulled ashore. As Kiri sang the sun-farewell, she thought of Mali singing in the village, and the link between them comforted her.

As she sat beside the water chewing a meal cake, a korlu cried, circling high against the darkening sky. Kiri slipped *within*, searching the land below through its eyes, seeking a path to the next lake, and the next. Something tugged at her memory. Would she come at last to the place where Ana and Yaro had found her, the place where her parents had left her?

A wave of loneliness swept over Kiri so suddenly that lake and sky blurred before her eyes. She fumbled for her story beads. Her fingers curled around a bead carved with the branches and trunk of a leafless tree. She heard again the slow *drip, drip, drip* of sap filling the bucket her mother had woven from bark and hung on a tree. Boiled down, the sap would sweeten Kiri's meal cakes and the hot, bitter broth her parents drank.

The taste of the sap was a sweet memory on her tongue, and her father's voice sang in her head, "Come rising, come rising, fill the tree, fill my bucket, feed my little one. Come rising, come rising. . . ."

He had loved her, her father. And he had gone away. They had both gone away.

"Why?" she asked aloud.

But there was no answer for her question.

Kiri's fingers tightened on the story bead until it cut into her skin. She sang the words to the song, but they sounded thin and forlorn in the empty evening, like the voice of a broken-winged bird.

She put the beads away and rolled up in her bedskins. One by one she watched the stars bloom until the sky was crowded with bright bursts of light.

Kiri dreamed. In the dream she stood at the edge of a great lake, the largest she had ever seen. The sun hovered above the water, although she could not remember calling it into the sky.

"It is the same sun that rises by the village," she told herself, "the same morning." But even in her dream she did not believe it.

Kiri, Kiri, voices called to her across the water, and a great longing rose up in her.

"Mother," she cried, "Father, is it you?" She started to paddle across the lake, but a wind sprang up, capsizing the abar and drowning the sound of her name.

Is it death who calls me?
Is it death who knows my name?

5

Kiri leaned on her paddle and studied the sky and the wide lake stretching beyond the bay. For five days she had paddled while the weather had held clear and bright. Now clouds gathered like ragged gray wings and came flapping toward her. Tenabi skimmed close to the choppy waters, seeking sheltered places. The reeds at the water's edge bent flat beneath the olo, the wind that came before a storm.

Should she wait here until the storm blew itself out? She could pull her abar up beneath the trees and make camp.

But no vision had spoken to her yet, and the meal cakes and dried meat were almost gone. Soon she would have to take time to search for food.

And Mali will be needing me, Kiri thought. Maybe the far side of this lake will be far enough to find my vision. Maybe I can cross before the storm breaks.

She pulled her abar down to the shore. It bobbled restlessly on the waves but steadied as Kiri climbed in. The wind blew against her, and she had to paddle hard to get free of the shore. When she rounded a rocky point into the open lake, the wind struck her full in the face, blowing at an angle to the white-capped waves. When she pointed the abar into the wind, the waves tossed her sideways.

Her hands tightened on her paddle, and she hunched her shoulders. She had never seen a wind like this before. It took all her strength to hold the abar against both wave and wind. The far shore of the lake was disappearing in a blanket of rain, and the clouds were closing in above her. If she tried to turn back toward shore, the waves could catch the abar broadside, overturning it.

Her heart pounded wildly as she remembered the dream, the voices calling her name and her abar capsizing. But here there were no voices except the roaring of the wind and the sudden sharp crack of thunder as lightning began to strike the water around her.

A wave washed over the front of the abar, soaking Kiri's bedskins. The abar settled deeper under the weight of wet skins, and another wave splashed in. Slowly the wind began to turn the abar crosswise to the climbing hills of water.

Kiri dug her paddle into the water and struggled to point the abar into the waves. But another wave washed in, and a gust of wind swept the abar sideways, overturning it.

The water was so cold it took Kiri's breath away. She struggled to the surface, gasping for air. Rain drove into her mouth, and her water-soaked clothes dragged her down.

As her head broke free of the water again, she searched frantically for the abar. Rain filled her eyes.

"Mali!" she cried as another wave washed over her.

Like a small flame in her mind came Kiri's memory of a day she had spent *within* a pelle. The sleek little animal had dived and splashed and floated in the water.

As she surfaced again, Kiri clung to that memory. The rain still beat against her face, but a different strength filled her arms and legs. Now the waves were hills to climb and slide along.

The wind was forcing her back to the shore from which she had set out. Again and again the waves carried her up, but all she could see were their white-capped tops. Her arms ached, and her breath began to come in gasps. At last a darker blur warned her that the shore was near. As the next wave carried her in, her foot caught between two rocks, so that the swell tossed her underwater. Kiri wrenched

her foot loose as another wave lifted her up. As it fell away, she felt earth beneath her fingers.

Wave after wave washed over her as she dragged herself toward the darkness of the forest. The wet earth pulled her down. She lay for a long time with her face pressed against the rocky ground.

Gradually the thunder died, and the pounding of the waves subsided. Rain still fell steadily from a gray sky. Kiri dragged herself to her knees and strained to see through the wet dimness. Her abar was nowhere in sight.

She could not stop shaking. Warm, she thought. I have to get warm.

Her fingers curled around the firestone in her belt pouch. When she pulled the stone out, it lay round and cold in her hand.

A fire, thought Kiri. Only a fire.

She would not think now of what would happen to her in strange country, without an abar, without supplies, with fierce white winter winging down toward her. If she could not get warm and dry before nightfall, nothing else would matter.

She struggled up, crying out as she put her weight on her hurt ankle. Dragging her foot, she staggered deeper under the trees. Even here rain had soaked the fallen branches and broken limbs.

A few dry leaves, Kiri told herself. That's all. Just a few dry leaves.

She found them a little way into the forest where

a tree trunk had blocked the fall of another tree, holding it partway above the ground. Under the thick trunk dry leaves clung to its branches, and the earth felt damp but not drenched. Kiri found a few dry twigs and a handful of leaves and gathered them into a pile. She struck her firestone until a spark leaped into the leaves. The steady drizzle of rain defeated it.

The next spark lit, flickered hopefully, and died before the leaves could catch. Kiri struck spark after spark, watching them skitter wildly across the ground. Finally she sank back on her heels, trembling. Would Mali know if she died here, alone and freezing?

In her mind's eye Kiri saw Mali standing before the fire-circle, lighting the ceremonial fire for the shortest day of light, the longest night. His voice as he struck sparks into the stack of wood sang in her mind: "Sun hears my song, wind hears my song, fire hears my song, comes dancing, comes dancing."

Like the warm, strong touch of Mali's hand, the words steadied Kiri. She bent over the tiny pile of branches and struck another spark.

"Fire comes dancing, comes dancing," she whispered through chattering teeth.

Light flickered through the leaves, caught, went out, caught again, and began to burn with a small, hesitant flame.

Kiri huddled close to the fire, feeding it leaf after

leaf until the branches began to blaze with a slender warmth. But the fire was more smoke than flame, and Kiri's clothes were too soaked to dry completely. In the end, she made a bed of leaves under the fallen tree and burrowed as deeply as she could against the night and the cold.

On the edge of sleep she thought she heard a voice calling her name.

"Mali," she answered wearily, "how will I ever get home to you now?"

In the place of singing waters
only my voice is silent.

6

Sunlight awakened Kiri. Around her the forest still dripped from yesterday's rain. High in the branches birds were singing, and a bright sun hung in a blue sky. Kiri blinked in the light, trying to make sense of the leaves hanging about her face. There had been the dream again, great rolling waves, the abar overturning. . . .

The memory of the storm flooded over her as she rolled out from under the tree. Her whole body ached. Pain pierced her ankle when she stood up. She had to lean against a tree to sing the sun-rejoicing.

The sun has come up before me, she thought. What would Mali say?

Once, as a child, she had asked him, "Will the sun come up if you do not call it?"

"The sun follows its own path, whether I call it

or not," he had told her. "We would be a poor people if we could not offer it welcome when it came."

But Mali was far away. Water and forest separated them, a five-day journey by abar. The only paths were the ones Kiri had followed between lake and river or lake and lake. The way home lay across water too wide, too bitterly cold to swim. Without an abar there was no way of returning to Mali.

Perhaps he was dying already. The thought of life without Mali rose up like a sudden wind, scattering her thoughts. Would he leave her, too, and go into that white empty silence where her parents had gone?

Kiri looked wildly around her. A tenabe circled, crying. *Within* the tenabe she would be safe, away from questions. Kiri slipped *within*.

The air was strong under her wings, lifting her into the sky. She caught a current of wind, riding it higher. Somewhere in the water below was a flicker that might be a fish. Something gleamed against the rocks along the shore. . . .

Kiri withdrew from the bird and narrowed her eyes against the dancing sunlight.

Only a dead tree, she told herself. But her heart began to thump faster as she limped to the edge of the sand and shaded her eyes with her hand. She could not be certain if the sun shone back off the bleached wood of a branch that had washed up onshore or off the smooth surface of an abar.

She found a stick to lean on and began to make her way through the tumbled rocks and tangled branches. She tripped and stumbled so often that in the end she felt she had crawled the whole length of the shore. Finally she lay on her stomach across a rock looking down on the wreck of her abar.

Built of slender strips of wood for lightness on the trail, the abar had been splintered and ripped by the battering waves. Part of one side was torn away, and the bow had broken apart so that the abar lay wedged in two pieces against the rocks. Any hope she had of repairing it died.

But her bedskins were still bound to the center thwart. She eased herself over the edge of the boulder and slid down until she felt the abar under her feet. Kneeling, she worked to untie the knots that bound the bedskins to the abar. Water had swelled the rope tight. Kiri bit her lip as she used her knife to cut the bedskins free. Every scrap of rope she could save would help her. Survival, she knew, could hang on the warmth of a fire or the sharpness of a knife.

Water had doubled the weight of the skins. When at last Kiri tugged one up onto the rock, she lay panting with the effort. She unrolled the bedskin. The meal cakes and meat stored inside were soaked. Kiri scooped up the soggy crumbs of meal cake, licking them off her fingers. Her stomach rumbled. Maybe the meat at least could be saved. She laid the strips out on the rock, then spread her bedskin out in the sun to dry.

She rested a moment before sliding down into the abar again. As she bundled up the second bedskin, something spilled out into the abar. Tomar's black pot. Traveling quickly, eating only meal cakes and dried meat, Kiri had not used the pot. Every morning she had carefully wrapped it in the bedskins. Now as it lay at her feet with the waves rippling around it, the pot seemed to belong to another world.

Kiri stared at the pot, remembering Tomar and her laughter; Ebba singing; Mali, who might be dying.

Would she ever see them again?

Kiri pushed the thought away. She would find a way back even if she had to wait for winter and the waters to freeze, even if she walked home over the ice.

But you have not yet had your vision, a voice whispered in her mind. How can you go back without it?

I sought my vision, she answered herself. And it brought me here, far from Mali, without an abar, without food. Now I must go back. Mali needs me. I can seek my vision again in the spring.

She stooped and tucked the bowl inside her

tunic. When she had finally spread both bedskins to dry in the sun, she lay exhausted on the boulder, feeling the smooth warm stone under her cheek.

That night she ate a few of the dried strips of meat she had salvaged. They had hardened again in the sun and made a sour, chewy meal. The meat would not last long, and the forest was far into autumn. Many of the trees and bushes were bare of fruit.

There are nuts, thought Kiri, and roots if I can dig them before the ground freezes. I can make snares.

Searching for food or setting snares would be easier once her foot healed.

Or I could heal it, Kiri thought. Maybe.

Huddled under a bush, watching the sky darken, she heard Mali's words so clearly that for an instant she thought he had spoken.

"To take on another's pain is one thing," he had told her. "To take on your own pain and heal it is a very great task indeed."

And I could not even go with Mali at Nikil's healing, Kiri thought. But if I cannot heal my ankle, who knows when I will ever get home again?

"I'm not afraid," she said aloud. But fear blew through her like a wintry wind.

I call to the wind,
but the wind will not speak.

7

While the moon shrank to a sliver thin as a knife blade, Kiri's days fell into a rhythm that began with the sun-rejoicing and ended in exhausted sleep. She welcomed the work. It was like a fire that she built, holding back at the edges of its light the fear that Mali might not live until she returned.

She had tried healing her ankle. Within a stone's throw of her camp she had found the healing herbs, ennis and arrel, the leaves of the arrel curled tight against frost. She had built a fire and sat beside it.

But at the first words of the healing song, she had felt an emptiness opening around her, cold and white as winter. *Kiri, Kiri,* a voice called.

The words of the song froze in Kiri's chest. She huddled by the fire, waiting for courage to begin again. The emptiness waited, too.

At last she had cut a strip from the hem of her tunic and bound her ankle tightly. It hurt, but she could still do what had to be done.

Using her knife, Kiri carefully pried apart the wooden strips and thwarts of the abar and built a wellan, thatching it with pine boughs and bundles of the dried grass that grew among the rocks at the water's edge. The wellan was small and had no room for a fire, but with her bedskins she would be warm enough. She built a small fire-circle just beyond the entrance, facing the lake.

From the inner bark of a fallen tree she braided rope and wove it into nets. With these she caught a few fish. Along the edge of the lake she dug shellfish and ate them, saving their shells to use for cups. She fashioned snares and set them along the trail between the lakes to catch small, unwary animals. In the forest she dug roots from the hard ground and dried them. She found a large, smooth rock and a smaller, round one that she could use for pounding the roots into flour.

Although hunger chewed at her constantly, Kiri always dried part of the meat from the few animals she snared, saving the narrow strips for her long walk back. The skins she scraped with a sharpened length of bone and stretched to cure, saving them to make warmer clothes.

Once, searching in the forest for branches to

strengthen her wellan, Kiri found a store of nuts that some skirre had hoarded.

"Forgive me, little brother," Kiri whispered as she caught up the edge of her tunic and filled it with half the nuts. "I know how hunger will hunt you this winter. But I am hungry, too."

Kiri was gathering firewood one morning when a faint whimper reached her ears. She stood still, listening, but the sound did not come again. Quietly she knelt down and looked into the underbrush. From the shadows two yellow eyes looked back at her.

In the darkness under the bushes Kiri could not tell what kind of animal it was. She slipped *within*.

Pain climbed her leg in a burning line. Fur stood up along her back, and she growled at a shadowy form outside the bushes.

Kiri withdrew and crouched back to think. The animal was wounded. If she could kill it, she would have meat.

But the memory of its pain burned in her. Mali would heal the pain, or try to, if he were here. But there was only Kiri, alone. Kiri peered again at the yellow eyes and saw that they were watching her.

"I will heal you," she whispered, "if I can."

Back in her camp Kiri filled Tomar's pot with water and put in her belt pouch the healing herbs that she had gathered but not used.

Her hands trembled as she gathered up an armload of firewood. She moved quietly as she neared the log where she had found the animal. Would it still be there? She eased the wood onto the ground and set the pot of water next to it. Through the branches yellow eyes watched her, unblinking.

Kiri built a small fire. When it was burning, she began to sing.

"Wind, hear my song. Wind, hear my name."

With her mind she reached out to the animal. Pain swept over her. She fought against it toward the bright, hot hurting.

But a great white emptiness yawned around her, swallowing the words of her song.

Kiri, Kiri, called a voice. She heard her own voice cry out as the emptiness swept over her.

Kiri opened her eyes. The ground was rough against her face. A hand, fingers dug into the earth, swam into focus near her eyes. It took a moment to realize that the fingers were her own.

Slowly the world took shape around her. Kiri sat up. The animal crouched under the bushes. When she entered *within,* its leg still burned. She had not healed it.

Tears filled her eyes. She blinked them back and pulled the pot of water into the dwindling fire. If she could not heal the wound, at least she could clean it.

When the water was hot, she stretched out on her stomach by the bushes. Two yellow eyes still watched her.

"Ahabe, friend," Kiri called quietly. At the word of command, the animal lay unmoving. Kiri wriggled under the branches to lay her hand on its fur. She could make out slender gray legs and pointed ears, a long, narrow muzzle. Thick gray fur covered the animal's back and sides, and his long, bushy tail curled around his feet.

A wolken. He would come past her knee if he stood on all four legs.

His left hind leg had a deep gash running across it. Kiri washed it carefully, singing softly to the wolken as she worked. His eyes never blinked as he watched her.

When she was done, she stroked his fur. It felt thick and coarse under her hand.

At last she backed out of the bushes and whispered, "Eloni." The word released the wolken from stillness. The yellow eyes closed slowly, and the wolken settled deeper into the leaves to sleep.

Kiri was almost asleep that night when something whispered in her mind. The wolken's wound had been long and straight, as though not teeth or claws but a spear point had torn his flesh. A spear meant hunters, and hunters might have an abar. Maybe they were somewhere close by. Kiri sat up under her shelter, hugging the bedskins.

If there were hunters, if she could find them, she would have a way home to Mali.

Kiri spent the next day collecting sticks and branches, piling them out on the flat rock where she stood each morning to sing the sun-rejoicing. She would light a fire when darkness fell. If there were hunters, they might see the flames and come to find her.

"Mali, I'm coming," she whispered. A cloud slipped over the sun. As Kiri watched, the shadow of the cloud crept slowly across the lake. Beneath it the water darkened, then brightened again as the cloud passed.

The wolken is like that, Kiri thought. She saw him in her mind's eye, fading into the shadows under the bushes, and she smiled. She knew what she would call him.

She found a werrel in one of her snares, and carried it, along with a pot of water, to the bush where she had found the wolken. In the darkness under the branches she could not see him.

"Cloud Shadow," she called softly. "Ahabe, friend." Gingerly she extended a hand. A cold, wet nose brushed her fingers.

Kiri entered *within*. The leg still burned, but the

wolken had not chewed away at it. She ran her hand lightly along the wound. The wolken growled softly, but he did not move. Kiri backed away and whispered, "Eloni," as she pushed the dead werrel under the bush. The wolken nosed it, and one paw moved to cover the werrel.

That night she piled the branches high, feeding the fire until it blazed like a beacon.

The moon rose and floated across the sky. Tenabi cried, and once Kiri heard the soft slosh of some animal wading into the lake to drink. But no one came to her fire. The wood burned down to embers, flickering like stars.

Tomorrow, Kiri thought as she rolled up in her bedskins. Tomorrow night the hunters will come.

Something wet brushed the back of her neck. Kiri rolled over in her bedskins and stared into two yellow eyes. I am dreaming, she told herself. But a warm body nestled against her, and a tongue licked her hand.

"Cloud Shadow," she whispered, stroking the wolken's neck. The animal rested his head with a sigh. All night as she slept, she could feel the warmth of Cloud Shadow's body next to hers.

For three more nights Kiri built a beacon fire. Each night Cloud Shadow slept beside her.

But no hunters came.

The earth breathes.
The wind is blowing, blowing.

8

Kiri awoke one night to a deep stillness. No wind blew through the bare branches. The lake lay still under a moonless sky. As Kiri listened, she heard a single sound, like the beat of the meeting drum or the first great crack when the ice breaks in spring. Kiri began to shake.

"Mali!" she cried.

Cloud Shadow lifted his head and howled, a high, eerie, mournful cry that dropped into silence.

The wind began to blow softly again. A great wave of love flooded over Kiri. She began to sob. Cloud Shadow whined and licked her face. Then the wave flowed past her, and Kiri was alone in her shelter with Cloud Shadow and the certain knowledge that Mali had died.

Kiri huddled in her shelter, dreading the sunrise. Finally the sky began to pale. Long streaks of red began to weave through the clouds. Kiri crouched next to Cloud Shadow, burying her face and hands in his thick fur. Soon she would have to walk out onto the rock and greet the day alone.

Alone. The word echoed inside of Kiri. "We go alone, but not alone," Mali had told her. But now he had left her, as her parents had left her in the snowy silence of the winter tent.

It could not be true. She must have dreamed it. When she sang the sun-rejoicing, she would know that Mali was alive, singing with her.

Kiri crawled past Cloud Shadow out of the shelter. Behind her she heard him stir and stretch to follow. Her breath rose in a little cloud as she stumbled across the rocky shore to the great flat rock where she had built the beacon fires.

"Sun, arise. Awake the day," Kiri began. Her own words echoed back across the water. No one sang with her.

"Mali, Mali!" she cried. "Who will know if I do not finish the song? See, already the sun is rising without my help. How can I go on if you are not here with me?"

Cloud Shadow leaned against her. Kiri knelt down and flung her arms around the wolken. Cloud Shadow nuzzled her arm. In silence Kiri watched the sun rise. Already dark clouds heavy with snow were scurrying to cover it. The coldness soaked into Kiri's bones, filling her up.

Crouched next to Cloud Shadow, she watched numbly until the wind whipped hard little pellets of ice against her face. Then she turned back to the shelter.

From inside the wellan she watched the storm spit a white covering over rocks and branches. The choppy black waters of the lake swallowed up the snow as though it had never been.

The wind rose in a thin, keening cry. Beneath it Kiri heard other voices.

"Do not be afraid," her father had said as another long-ago storm had howled outside the winter tent. Kiri had huddled next to him in the strong comfort of his arms.

"It is the wind who speaks," her mother had said. "When the wind is silent, we will hunt again. And there will be new skins to wrap a small one in." She had smiled at Kiri.

Kiri tightened her grip on Cloud Shadow. Against the high voice of the wind Kiri raised her own voice in the song for the dead. The storm caught up her words and scattered them across the driving snow.

All day Kiri watched snow claim the land. Images floated across her mind one by one.

Ana, stooping down in the snow to study the tracks of a derek.

Ebba, leaning against her to learn the words of a new song.

Nikil, tilting her head back in the sunlight to watch a flight of tenabi.

Tomar, her long brown fingers patiently kneading the clay. Kiri wanted to reach out and touch the fine coating of dried clay on those hands, wanted to hear her friend laugh again.

How could she go back to them without her vision? The people had need of a healer, and she had nothing to give them. Who would help them now?

Darkness fell early, and the lake swallowed it up, too. From her shelter Kiri watched as the blackness of sky and water met. She and the wolken seemed to be the only ones left in the world.

She spoke aloud to hear her own voice in the silence.

"I will stay here with you, Cloud Shadow."

She would not sing the sun-rejoicing or the sun-farewell any longer. They were a part of her life with Mali, a singer's life, a life she had no claim to any longer.

A voice in the wind . . . .
Who is it calls my name?

9

Ice thickened on the lake, and Kiri began to melt snow for water. She cut two thin saplings and bent them back on themselves so that the ends touched. In between she wove long strips of hide to make snowshoes. It was still early winter, and the snow crust had not yet formed. With her snowshoes Kiri did not sink so deeply into the snow.

Every few days Cloud Shadow would bring her some small, dead animal. The snows around the wellan grew covered with his tracks, the print of one paw twisted from the scar running down his leg.

In the evenings she took out her beads and told the wolken, bead by bead, the stories she had heard in the winter tent. Life in the village seemed long ago, a winter dream, a song whose words she could no longer remember.

Something was wrong. Kiri knew it even before she opened her eyes. Next to her in the darkness Cloud Shadow growled low in his throat. She reached out a hand to quiet him and felt the hair on his back standing stiffly up.

"What do you hear?" she whispered. She shoved aside the branches that she pulled over the entrance each night. Snow was falling outside, thick and white, blanketing everything. Cloud Shadow rose, crouching low to the ground. Kiri tried to tighten her grip on him, but his fur grew so thickly that her fingers slid away. Cloud Shadow slipped outside.

After a few moments the wolken returned, licking snowflakes from his fur. He settled next to her, and Kiri lay down again, reassured. Whatever it was, Cloud Shadow had chased it away.

The snow still fell at sunrise, and in the soft white drifts Kiri could find no sign of an intruder. The wolken stayed in camp while Kiri checked her snares. They were empty, and Kiri dusted over her tracks with a branch as she walked back to her shelter.

At the edge of the trees, she stopped. Someone was standing in her campsite, facing away from her. Her heart leaped when she saw the spear. A hunter.

She opened her mouth to call out. Then she saw how the hunter's head turned from side to side as though searching for something. Kiri looked, too. On the far edge of her campsite stood Cloud Shadow, almost invisible under the trees.

The hunter saw the wolken at the same instant. He raised his spear.

"No!" Kiri screamed.

Startled, the hunter turned toward her, and out of a gaunt face Garen looked back at Kiri.

His eyes narrowed when he saw her, and he swung back to fling his spear at the wolken. With a *thwuck* the spear buried itself in a tree behind Cloud Shadow. The wolken faded like smoke into the forest.

"Cloud Shadow!" Kiri cried. As the wolken disappeared, Garen shouted with rage and took a step forward. His knees buckled, and he fell headlong in the snow.

Kiri wanted to run after Cloud Shadow, but Garen's body held her back. She went to him and tried to roll him over.

He turned limply in the snow. His eyelids were closed, and Kiri could see how his eyes were sunken into his face and his cheekbones stood out. He looked thin and weary and cold.

Kiri crouched back on her heels, anger and fear twisting inside of her. Was Garen the hunter who

had wounded Cloud Shadow? If she kept Garen at her camp, Cloud Shadow would not return. But she could not leave him behind to go search for the wolken. Garen had pushed himself to exhaustion and needed healing.

Could she heal him?

Hard behind this thought came another: Do I want to?

Kiri rocked back and forth on her heels in the snow, looking down at Garen's thin, dark face. Mali's words came back to her: "If he cannot find his path he will have need of me—or of you."

Mali would have healed Garen.

But Mali was gone. And Garen might die without help.

"Mali," Kiri whispered. Her throat tightened, but she swallowed her grief. Mali was not here, but she was. If Garen had any hope, she was that hope. She would try for Mali, if not for Garen.

Kiri stood and grasped Garen's ankles. He did not even have snowshoes. She could feel the bones of his legs and the coldness of his skin.

Kiri pulled Garen over to the shelter and rolled him onto her bedskins, wrapping him snugly inside. By the entrance she built a fire and filled Tomar's pot with snow. As it melted, she dug in her pouch for the unused bundle of healing herbs. Then she settled herself next to the fire and waited while her breathing deepened. It took a long time. She kept hearing the soft thud of the spear hitting wood, kept seeing Cloud Shadow as he disappeared among the trees. At last she stilled her thoughts, and her breathing slowed.

"Help me, Mali," Kiri whispered. Softly she began to sing.

A great white emptiness blossomed around her, drawing her into its heart.

Kiri cried out and pulled back from Garen. Her whole body trembled. She could not go *within* to heal him. Something waited for her there, something that knew her name.

But Garen might die if she failed.

Garen, who had killed the werrel.

Garen, who had driven Cloud Shadow away.

Garen, who was in need of healing.

Garen, who had always been alone, as she was alone.

Kiri reached out and laid a hand on his wrist, bone cold under her fingers. She closed her eyes, drew a deep breath, and began to sing again.

"Wind, hear my song—"

Cold fire burned along her arms and legs. *Kiri.* A voice called her name, drawing her down to somewhere empty and white.

She gripped Garen's arm tightly and continued to sing.

"Wind, hear my name—"

The emptiness opened inside her, all around her.

Vast and white and never ending, it swallowed her up.

Somewhere a voice was singing. Kiri knew it for her own voice. But it did not matter anymore. Nothing mattered. She was nothing, drifting in nothing.

Kiri, the voices called. *Kiri*.

And suddenly there was stillness.

She could still hear her own voice singing far away, but here, at the center, was a quiet as vast and white as winter. Here *within* Garen, beyond the edge of his pain, was the place of healing that Mali had told her about.

She was not alone in the center. At first she thought it was Mali standing beside her. Then she made out the shadowy form of a young man, his hair held back by a woven gray band. Kiri could see clearly the knife in his hand. In the palm of his other hand he held the small, carved shape of a tenabe.

Kiri knew without thinking what to do. She let Garen's weariness and the coldness in his hands and arms and legs flow into her. A wind swept her along, carrying the pain out to the empty sky.

Empty, empty, Garen was empty, she was empty, too. The healing winds blew it all away.

Kiri's heart rose as she neared the end of the song. She sang the last words, then reached to crumble the herbs over the water.

87

Shivering with cold, she huddled over the fire. A warmth inside her spread slowly out toward her numb fingers and feet. She knew that Garen's body would recover.

"Mali," she whispered above the singing in her heart.

The wind, comes the wind.
Over the frozen lake it comes.

10

▶▶◆◀◀

It was nearly evening before Garen opened his
eyes. Kiri sat beside him, tending the fire. He
frowned when he saw her and tried to rise but fell
back onto the bedskins.

"Here, drink this." She offered him the bowl of
water and leaves. Garen tried to turn his head away,
but he was too weak to resist.

Neither did he refuse the small bits of meat that
Kiri fed him one by one. When he had finished,
he lay back and closed his eyes. Weariness settled
over his face. Kiri saw that he had fallen asleep.

"Now I will go find Cloud Shadow," she told
herself. But she did not leave the shelter. Instead
she watched Garen's chest rise and fall with each
shallow breath.

Kiri reached out to touch him. No emptiness
opened around her. No bone-chilling cold flowed

into her. His arm was only an arm, warm under her
fingers.

I have healed him, she thought.

From where she sat by the entrance of the shelter,
Kiri could see moonlight shining in a long, gleaming
ribbon across the ice. Something was moving along
that path. Kiri narrowed her eyes to see better.

"Cloud Shadow!" she cried, leaping up. Her feet
sank into the snow as she scrambled toward the
shore. But when she reached the rock, she realized
that the wolken crossing the ice toward her could
not be Cloud Shadow. This wolken was changing,
growing in size until his eyes were level with Kiri's.
Moonlight shone through the edges of his coat, so
that he seemed to wear a covering of light.

Kiri stood rooted to the rock, trembling.

"It is a dream," she told herself.

But the wolken stopped in front of her, so close
that she could feel his breath, warm in the frigid
air. He looked into her eyes, and although he did
not speak, Kiri heard his words inside her.

Healer, your people are waiting.

Kiri held out her hands, palms up, fingers outstretched.

"What gift can I bring them?" she asked aloud.

*Singer to the sun, caller of the wind, your power is your
song. I name you Amarra, she who speaks with the wind.*

Amarra. Kiri turned the name over in her mouth,
tasting it.

Your people are waiting, the wolken said again. Then he turned and trotted back along the path of moonlight until Kiri could no longer see him in the trail of shining silver.

Kiri stood on the rock for a long time, shivering in the wintry night. Were the villagers waiting for her as she had waited once in a winter tent? Could she go again among the voices of their pain? Could she bring them a gift of healing?

Garen needed me, Kiri thought. Without me he would have died in the cold. Cloud Shadow needed me, too.

The moon set, and the constellations swam slowly across the sky. People flickered like stars before Kiri's eyes.

Ana and Yaro, who had brought her to the village. Mali, who had loved her. Tomar, who heard the voices of clay. Ebba, her face alight with the treasures she brought to share. Nikil, her fingers dancing in and out of the loom. Garen, who slept a healing sleep. Kiri's people.

At last the darkness of the eastern sky began to fade. When the sun raised a pale orange head above the horizon, Kiri lifted her arms and began to sing.

A wolken it was who named me.
A wolken it was who gave me power.

11

▶▶◆◀◀

For two days Garen slept, waking only to drink the hot broth or to eat the small pieces of meat Kiri offered. She left him only to sing the sun-rejoicing and farewell or to check her snares, afraid that if he awoke alone, he would leave to search for Cloud Shadow. When she checked her snares, she would watch for signs of the wolken, but she saw none.

"Cloud Shadow," she would call softly, but he did not come.

On the third morning Garen was awake when Kiri returned to the shelter. Neither of them spoke as she built a fire and began to melt snow.

"Your vision has come," Garen said abruptly as she sprinkled a few dried berries into the water. His voice was thin and high.

Kiri looked up, startled, then nodded.

Garen's face tightened. Thinking he was in pain, Kiri reached out to touch him, but he brushed her hand aside.

"Did you seek your vision?" she asked.

Garen turned away. Kiri saw a tear slide down his face. He wiped it angrily away.

"I waited for my vision," he told her. "I did not even hunt for food. But nothing spoke, not last time, not this time." His voice was bitter. "And then . . . I found the wolken."

Kiri stirred the broth so fiercely that a little splashed out, sizzling in the fire.

You followed me, she thought. You were the hunter who wounded Cloud Shadow.

But she would not say the wolken's name aloud.

As though she had spoken, Garen answered, "I thought if I could bring back a derek or a wolken, it would prove I was a hunter."

His pain at losing the wolken wove in and out of Kiri's own. Her hands trembled, and she laid them on her knees to keep them still.

"And would you have been a hunter then?" she asked.

"No!" Garen shouted. He dropped his face in his hands, his shoulders shaking.

Kiri wanted to run from Garen's despair into the stillness of the trees. But she was not just Kiri any longer. She was Amarra. And Amarra would not run away.

She looked down at her hands where they lay on her knees, fingers curled. "If you would know your vision," she told Garen softly, "you must listen."

"I listen!" he shouted. "But nothing speaks to me."

"You listen only to hear what you want to hear," Kiri told him. "I know," she added as he started to argue, "because I did not want to listen either."

"You? You've always known what your vision will say."

"But I did not want to hear it," she told him. "I wanted only to hear it say something else, anything else, so that I would not have to be a healer. So that I could go back to—to Mali." It hurt to say his name, but she went on, "I did not want to hear my vision speak and name me healer."

"But it spoke," Garen said.

Kiri looked down at her hands. A healer's hands now. "It spoke because of you," she told him. "Because you came. Because I healed you. . . . I thank you."

Garen was silent.

"Will you seek your vision now?" she asked. "Will you listen?"

Garen lay back on the bedskins and turned his face away. He was quiet so long Kiri thought he had fallen asleep.

"Help me," he said at last.

Kiri remembered the shadowy figure of the healing and the carving in his hand. There had been power in that carving. It had helped to heal Garen. Kiri wanted to lay her hand on Garen's arm and tell him, "You have a gift. I have seen it."

But she could not. He must find his own way to his vision. Instead she pulled the bedskins closer around him and said, "I kept you from dying. To find your vision you must heal yourself."

Mali's words.

Garen's hope stabbed through her. "What do you mean?" he asked.

"Only what Mali said once," she answered, hearing how her voice shook. "And now he is dead, and I have my vision, and I do not know if I can go back to the village without him."

"Mali is dead?"

Kiri nodded, and Garen bowed his head. When he looked up, he said, his voice low, "Then you are healer now. And I have not yet thanked you for saving my life." He held out his hand, palm up.

Kiri placed her hand over his. The skin of his fingers was cracked from the cold.

"What will you do now?" he asked.

"The lakes are frozen," she said. "I will go back. What will you do?"

She held her breath, waiting for his answer. Could she go back to the village if it meant leaving Garen alone to search out Cloud Shadow?

"If you can listen, so will I," he replied. "If I hunt, it will be for food or for visions. I will not hunt the wolken again."

Kiri rolled up Tomar's bowl and half the food into a bedskin. Garen helped her to strap it on her back. He was strong enough to get around on his own again. It was time for Kiri to return to the village.

"Go well, Kiri," Garen said. He held out his hand. On his palm lay a carved bead. "Take it," he told her.

Kiri touched the bead. Carved in the wood was the body of a wolken, its tail curling around the bead to end by its nose.

For an instant Kiri saw again the young man of the healing, standing in Garen's shadow. When she blinked, he was gone. Carefully she untied her string of beads and slipped the new one on.

"Go well, Garen," she told him. "I will see you back at the village."

The snow lay deep under the trees, but Kiri's snowshoes kept her from sinking. Patterns of bird tracks dotted the snow, and once the deep prints of a derek crossed the trail. But Kiri saw no sign of Cloud Shadow. All day she walked along trails and across ice-covered lakes. At evening she scooped out a shallow cave in the snow under the shelter of an evergreen tree and curled up in her bedskin.

In the darkness her fingers felt for her story beads and found the wolken bead. Already a song was shaping itself in her mind.

"In the wind he comes, in the shadows he comes, smoke-colored, wolken-friend . . ." Kiri sang softly.

That night she dreamed of the winter tent, where she had crouched, waiting for her parents' return. Voices called out to her. This time they called, *Amarra, Amarra.*

The door flap of the tent fell open, and her mother and father entered. With a glad cry Kiri flung herself on them.

"Don't leave me," she cried, and they held her close and spoke in her mind, *We have never left you, Kiri, Amarra, little one. You go alone, but not alone.*

Inside the tent it felt warm and safe. Kiri's parents lay down beside her. The fur of their clothes felt soft and thick, like a wolken's. She slept content.

When Kiri awoke in the morning, she found the tracks of two wolken in the snow outside her cave. One of the paw prints twisted inward.

"Cloud Shadow," she called. But he did not come.

Looking at the footprints, Kiri knew that the wolken had gone back to his own kind in the forest. But her heart sang within her, Cloud Shadow,

Cloud Shadow. It was enough to know that the wolken was all right. And that he was still her friend.

As she reached into her belt pouch for a strap to tie up her bedskins, Kiri's fingers closed around Ebba's stone. Ebba would have new treasures to show her. Perhaps by now the villagers would be eating from Tomar's pots and bowls. And Nikil could weave for Kiri the red band of a singer to wear around her forehead.

Kiri's heart lifted as she shouldered her pack and fastened on her snowshoes. The wolken tracks crossed and recrossed the trail ahead. Somewhere a korlu called.

Kiri's feet moved to a silent rhythm, and she started to sing as she followed the path through the snow-covered trees.

> *"Comes the wind to my singing,*
> *comes the wind to my singing.*
>
> *Wind now begins to sing,*
> *wind now begins to sing.*
>
> *The wind is singing.*
> *My name it is singing.*
>
> *The earth breathes.*
> *The wind is blowing, blowing."*

GLOSSARY

▶▶◆◀◀

abar—a long, light slender boat made of wood.

ahabe—a word of power, used to command stillness.

arrel—an herb with long, leafy fronds, used in healing.

bloodberry—a dark-red berry that grows on thorny bushes and is useful in healing, especially cuts, wounds, and bruises.

derek—a large, long-legged animal hunted for both its meat and its hide.

eloni—a word of power used to release from stillness.

ennis—an herb with small, pale-blue flowers useful in healing.

feverleaf—a small gray herb with pointed leaves; a tea made by boiling the leaves is useful in treating fever.

full moon—a round yellow fruit with a sweet taste and small, crescent-shaped seeds.

korlu—a woodland bird with a sharp cry from which it gets its name.

olo—the wind that usually precedes stormy weather.

pela berries—small red berries that can be dried and chewed to relieve stomach pains.

pelle—a dark-furred water animal with webbed feet that lives along the shores of rivers and lakes.

skirre—a small, ground-burrowing animal that eats nuts, seeds, and berries.

tenabe (pl. tenabi)—a diving bird with a harsh cry that nests along the reedy shores of lakes.

wellan—a dwelling place made of bent saplings covered with reeds, skins, or blankets. Small wellans are used for sleeping, the large common wellan for taking meals together.

werrel—a small, thick-furred animal whose skin is white in winter and changes to mottled brown in summer. A bedskin of soft werrel fur is a common birth gift for a new baby.

wolken—an animal with slender legs, bushy tail, pointed nose, and keen eyesight and hearing.